*This story was inspired by the old Cornish legend
of Tom Bawcock. It is dedicated with affection
to my neighbours and friends,
the people and cats of Mousehole.*
A.B.

*For Sebastian Walker
with love*
N.B.

First published 1990 by Walker Books Ltd
87 Vauxhall Walk, London SE11 5HJ

This edition published 2006

10 9 8 7 6 5 4 3 2

Text © 1990 Antonia Barber

Illustrations © 1990 Nicola Bayley

The right of Antonia Barber and Nicola Bayley to be identified as
author and illustrator respectively of this work has been asserted by
them in accordance with the Copyright, Designs and Patents Act 1988

Printed in China

British Library Cataloguing in Publication Data:
a catalogue record for this book is available from the British Library

ISBN-13: 978-1-4063-0222-6
ISBN-10: 1-4063-0222-8

www.walkerbooks.co.uk

THE MOUSEHOLE CAT

WRITTEN BY

ILLUSTRATED BY

Antonia Barber · *Nicola Bayley*

WALKER BOOKS
AND SUBSIDIARIES

LONDON · BOSTON · SYDNEY · AUCKLAND

*A*t the far end of England, a land of rocks and moorland stretches itself out into a blue-green sea. Between its high headlands lie tiny sheltering harbours where the fishing boats hide when the winter storms are blowing.

One of these harbours is so small and the entrance between its great stone breakwaters is so narrow that fishermen called it "the Mousehole".

The people who lived in the cottages around the harbour grew fond of the name and they call their village Mousehole to this day.

They say it in the Cornish way, "Mowzel", but you may say it as you choose.

Once there lived in the village a cat whose name was Mowzer.

She had an old cottage with a window overlooking the harbour, an old rocking-chair with patchwork cushions and an old fisherman named Tom.

Mowzer had had many kittens in her time but they had all grown up and left home.

Her eldest son kept the inn on the quayside. It was noisy and smoky and his man had once spilled beer on Mowzer's head as he was drawing a pint.

So she did not go there very often.

One of her daughters kept the shop on the corner. It was busy and crowded and her lady had once stepped on Mowzer's tail as she was weighing out some vegetables.

So she did not go there very often either.

Sometimes Mowzer felt that her children had not trained their people properly.

Her own pet, old Tom, was very well behaved. He never spilled the cream when he was filling her saucer. He always stoked the range to a beautiful golden glow. He rocked the rocking-chair at just the right speed. He knew the exact spot behind her left ear where Mowzer liked to be tickled. What was more, he never wasted his time drawing pints of beer or weighing out vegetables.

When he was not looking after Mowzer he passed the day in the most useful way possible. He took his little boat through the narrow opening between the great breakwaters, out into the blue-green sea, and caught fish for Mowzer's dinner.

Mowzer was very partial to a plate of fresh fish.
In fact she never ate anything else. But she liked a little variety.

So, on Mondays they made morgy-broth,
Mowzer's favourite fish stew.
On Tuesdays they baked hake and topped it with
golden mashed potatoes.
On Wednesdays they cooked kedgeree with
delicious smoked ling.
On Thursdays they grilled fairmaids,
a mouth-watering meal.
On Fridays they fried launces with a knob
of butter and a squeeze of lemon.
On Saturdays they soused scad with
vinegar and onions.
And on Sundays they made star-gazy pie
with prime pilchards in pastry.

All in all, Mowzer's days passed very pleasantly.

Then one year there came a terrible winter. At the far end of England the blue-green sea turned grey and black.

The Great Storm-Cat is stirring, thought Mowzer as she watched at her window. The wind whined like a wild thing about the high headlands. It came hunting the fishing boats in their hidden harbours. When the Great Storm-Cat is howling, thought Mowzer, it is best to stay snug indoors by a friendly fire.

The sea drew itself up into giant waves and flung itself against the great breakwaters. All along the coast of Cornwall, the stone walls stood the shock.

Then the sea sucked up its strength again and roared right over them, sinking the sailing boats in their home havens. But it could not get into the Mousehole.

Mowzer watched as the Great Storm-Cat clawed with his giant cat's paw through the gap in the harbour wall. But it was too small.

He snarled and leaped up at the great breakwater under the lowering sky. But it was too high.

The fishing boats sat safe as mice in their own mousehole. But they could not get out.

And because the fishermen could not fish, there was no more food.

They ate up the few vegetables that were left in their storm-wracked gardens. They ate up the salted pilchards that were left in the cellars.

Mowzer hated vegetables and the pilchards were too salty for her taste.

Soon there was nothing left. The cats and their people grew very hungry.

Mowzer sat by her window, staring out at the storm, and thought longingly of morgy-broth and star-gazy pie.

Every day the fishermen gathered on the quayside and sometimes they would try to take a boat out through the Mousehole. But always the Great Storm-Cat lay in wait for them and they were lucky to escape with their lives.

Then at last one evening, as old Tom sat with Mowzer on his knee, she felt him take a deep sigh.

"Mowzer, my handsome," he said, for he was a courteous and well-spoken man, "Mowzer, my handsome, it will soon be Christmas, and no man can stand by at Christmas and see the children starve.

"Someone must go fishing come what may, and I think it must be me. It cannot be the young men, for they have wives and children and mothers to weep for them if they do not return. But my wife and parents are dead long since and my children are grown and gone."

Mowzer purred to tell him that she understood, for it was the same with her.

"I shall go out tomorrow, Mowzer, my handsome," said the old man, "and I shall not come back without a catch."

Mowzer purred louder to tell him that she would go with him.

For he was only a man, she thought, and men were like mice in the paws of the Great Storm-Cat.

Besides, she knew that if he did not come back, she would not much care to live in her cottage without him. There would be no one to pour the cream or stoke up the range or rock the rocking-chair. There would be no one in all the world who knew just where she liked to be tickled behind her left ear.

"Tomorrow night, Mowzer, my handsome," he said, "we shall eat morgy-broth, baked hake, ling and launces, fairmaids, soused scad *and* star-gazy pie!"

Then Mowzer purred as if she would burst to tell him that she loved him more than any of these things.

The next morning they set out very early, before the others were waking. Before they went, Tom stoked up the old range and damped it down so that it would burn steadily until they returned. Then he hung a lamp in the window so that it would shine out across the harbour and light their way.

As they reached the quayside, Mowzer looked back through the wind and rain, and thought how warm and welcoming the window looked.

Soon their little boat was crossing the harbour towards the Mousehole gap and the voice of the Great Storm-Cat rose all around them like a giant caterwauling.

As she listened to his wailing, Mowzer felt a sudden strange sadness for him. How lonely he must be, she thought, endlessly hunting the men-mice in the deeps of darkness, and never returning to the rosy glow of a red-hot range.

And her kind heart was moved to comfort him.

Many a tom-cat had Mowzer tamed in her time with the sweetness of her singing. Now she lifted her head and sang like a siren, joining her call with the cry of the Great Storm-Cat.

And so it was that he was taken off guard as the little boat made its bid for freedom. Soothed by the sweetness of Mowzer's serenade, the Great Storm-Cat paused in his prowling and pulled back his giant cat's paw for a mere moment. Swiftly the little boat passed through the Mousehole and out into the open sea.

Then the Great Storm-Cat played with them as a cat plays with a mouse. He would let them loose for a little as they fought their way towards the fishing grounds. Then down would come his giant cat's paw in a flurry of foam and water. But he did not yet strike to sink them, for that would have spoiled his sport.

When they reached the fishing grounds the sea was so rough that it was hard to put out the nets.

"I fancy you must sing again, Mowzer, my handsome," said Tom, "for your voice seems to soothe the sea like the sirens of old."

So Mowzer sang again, longer and louder than she had ever sung before. Indeed, old Tom was forced to block up his ears so that her siren-song should not distract him from the business of fishing.

And again, the Great Storm-Cat paused in his play and sang with her until the nets were safely shot.

All day they fished in a seething sea. The waves were so high and the clouds so low that they soon lost sight of the shore.

And all the time the Great Storm-Cat played with the little boat, striking it and then loosing it, but never quite sinking it. And whenever his claws grew too sharp, Mowzer would sing to him to soften the edge of his anger.

As evening came down they hauled in the nets. Into the belly of the boat tumbled ling and launces, scad, hake and fairmaids; enough fish for a whole cauldron of morgy-broth; enough pilchards for half a hundred star-gazy pies.

"Mowzer, my handsome, we are all saved," said old Tom, "if we can but bring this haul home to harbour."

But Mowzer knew that the Great Storm-Cat would strike when he saw them run for the shelter of the Mousehole.

She knew that the game serves only to sharpen the appetite for the feast to follow. It is his meal or mine, thought Mowzer, as she looked at the floundering fish in the belly of the boat. Blue, green and silver, they glistened in the greyness.

It made her mouth water to look at them.

As she thought of the morgy-broth murmuring on top of the range, the star-gazy pie growing golden in the oven, Mowzer began to purr.

And her purring rose like a hymn to home above the noise of the Great Storm-Cat's howling.

Such music had not reached the ears of the Great Storm-Cat since the dawn of Time, for when do cats purr out in the wind and the darkness?

Puzzled, he paused in his howling, bending his ear to catch the strange sound. It seemed to him that he had once heard such a song long before, when he was no more than a Storm-Kitten.

The Great Storm-Cat grew quiet: gone was his hunger for hunting, for making his meal of the mice-men.

Only the pleasure of the purring remained.

Then the Great Storm-Cat began to purr with Mowzer, and as the soft sound grew, the winds waned and the waves weakened.

Night fell, and the little boat sailed back across a slackening sea.

As they came in sight of home, a strange sight met their eyes. The whole village of Mousehole was shining with light and lanterns gleamed along both arms of the harbour.

For when the people of Mousehole had woken to find old Tom's

boat missing and a light left in his window, they knew that he had gone out to find fish for them, or to perish on the deep water.

All day they had watched and waited, staring out into the cloud-wracked sea, but they could see no sign of him.

And when night fell, the women went home and set candles in all their windows and every man lit his lantern and went down to the harbour walls.

As they waited and watched, they saw that the wind was dying and that the sea was growing calm.

The dark clouds lifted and a thin moon shone out between them. And in the light of the thin moon, they saw a small boat coming and behind it came the smallest, tamest Storm-Kitten of a wind.

As old Tom and Mowzer came through the Mousehole gap, a sudden breeze caught them, a tiny, playful cat's paw, like a gesture of farewell.

There was a great deal of
cooking in Mousehole that night.
The people made a whole
cauldron of morgy-broth. They baked
hake, cooked kedgeree, grilled fairmaids,
fried launces, soused scad.
They baked half a hundred star-gazy pies.
Then, people and cats, they
feasted together, until the hunger was
no more than a memory.

And every year since that day, at the inn on the quayside, the people of Mousehole hold a fish-feast on the night before Christmas Eve and raise their glasses to the memory of old Tom.

And every year, in the yard at the back of the inn, the cats of Mousehole gather and raise a great howling to the memory of old Mowzer.

And every year, folk come from all over Cornwall at Christmas time, to see Mousehole lit up with a thousand lights, shining their message of hope and a safe haven to all those who pass in peril of the sea.